Map *of the* Farm

Published by Willow Creek Press
P.O. Box 147, Minocqua, Wisconsin 54548
Designed by Donnie Rubo

Photo Credits; p5 © Lynn M. Stone; p7 © Lynn M. Stone; p12 © Sharon Eide / Elizabeth Flynn;
p13 © Terry Wild / Terry Wild Studio, Inc.; p15 © Sharon Eide / Elizabeth Flynn;
p16-17 © Sharon Eide / Elizabeth Flynn; p18 © Terry Wild / Terry Wild Studio, Inc.;
p24 © Kent Dannen; p25-27 © Terry Wild / Terry Wild Studio, Inc.;
p29 © Sharon Eide / Elizabeth Flynn; p30-31 © Bob Langrish; p32-33 © Richard Hamilton Smith

Printed in the United States

Secret of the Pasture

A CHILDREN'S ADVENTURE TALE

WILLOW CREEK PRESS

That morning on the farm, Piglet
knew something was wrong.

pssst.

Piglet peeked through sleepy eyes for
his friend Belle, the spotted horse,
who slept in the stable next to him.

"Belle, where are you?" asked Piglet.
But there was no answer.

Piglet looked everywhere. Belle was not
in the stable. Where could she be?

Piglet quickly stepped outside into the bright morning sun looking for Belle.

"Uncle Boar, have you seen Belle?" asked Piglet. "I don't know where she's gone!"

"Sorry," oinked Uncle Boar, "but I've been busy taking my morning mud bath. Let's ask the rest of the farm animals for help."

Uncle Boar lifted his head and
snorted as loud as he could,

"Hey everyone! Belle is gone!
We must all try to find her!"

"I can help," crowed the rooster.

cockl

doodle-doo

"I will cockle-doodle-doo and cockle-doodle-doo
as a signal for Belle to come home."

The baby chicks
also helped.
They looked high ...

...and low

…while the ducks looked left and right.

The bunnies sniffed the air hoping for a scent of Belle.

"And we can help too,"
cried the lambs.

"We'll go and look for
Belle in the north pasture."

The cow mooed…

moooo

The geese honked...

and the turkey gobble, gobble, gobbled.

Piglet looked across...

down...

and all around.

But still Belle could not be found.
And Piglet worried even more.

"She must have wandered off the farm and
may be lost or hurt somewhere," fretted Piglet.

"The countryside is so big,
how are we to find her?"

"I have an idea," barked the dog.
"I will climb up to the top of my
house and look for Belle up there."

But the dog could not see
Belle from the top of his house.

"I have a better idea," squeaked the mouse.
"We'll ask the kitty to climb a tall tree
and look for Belle from up there."

"But I'm afraid," said kitty.
"I'm so little and the tree is so tall."

But kitty was very brave and used his little claws to crawl high up the tree.

He nestled onto a tall branch
and looked far into the distance.

"I think I see something in the pasture,
next to the big fence," he mewed softly.

Hearing this, Piglet ran over to the south pasture as fast as his little legs would let him and peeked over the big fence afraid of what he might see.

Piglet could hardly believe what he was seeing.

"Hello Piglet," said Belle, sounding very tired but very happy. "Meet my brand new daughter."

Belle licked the little filly and nudged her until she stood on her hooves for the very first time.

"Thank you, Piglet, and thank everyone
for caring so much about me.

My daughter and I are lucky to have
so many friends on this farm!"

"Come on, little Belle. Let's go meet
all your new friends on the farm."

The
End

North Pasture

Old Barn

Kitty's Big Tree

South Pasture